The Condition of Language

Tzu Yu Allison Lin

Acknowledgements

I want to thank Mr. Michael Song, the President of Showwe Publisher (Taipei, Taiwan), for his encouragement and his thoughtfulness. My thanks also go to Irene Cheng and Lestat Yin for making this book possible.

The Condition of Language

Preface

The initial idea of writing such a book on the condition of language comes from a question, which was asked by Jean-Paul Sartre in his book, *What is Literature?* In fact, Sartre truly wanted to ask himself and the readers, this essential question - 'What is Writing'?

In Sartre's *Words*, again, he mentioned the way in which

Charles Schweitzer was 'amazed' (Sartre 89) by the French language. In some ways, Schweitzer did not consider himself 'as a writer' - he 'played' with the language, and yet, 'had not quite made it his own' (Sartre 89).

Sartre's words indicate that to write in a specific language - as a writer - firstly one has to feel and to appreciate the sophistication of that particular language. Secondly, one needs to make this language his or her own, in order to make it alive in a written form.

Literature is not all about a play of a language, or a linguistic game. The written pages are not only a representation of the black and the white; the verbal and the visual. A writer somehow does not only write a book. He or she - most importantly - lives a book. The text itself does not only represent the condition of language - rather, it does represent the condition of one's own self.

Allison Lin

Gaziantep 2021

The Condition of Language

· Contents ·

1

Seeing Nature and the Cities

In this research, I read several literary texts through the lens of scenes of Nature and different cities. With perspectives of seeing works of art in culture and humanity, a better understanding towards the true meanings of these selected literary texts can be revealed. These literary texts are selected and aimed to observe the relation between Nature and culture, Nature and the cities, animals and the human beings, in a way in which human beings can find freedom and the meaning of life through the inspiration of Nature, as humanity can be expressed by artistic forms and narratives. Works of painting and works of photography in literary forms - namely, novels, poems, short stories, and dramatic plays - will be appreciated and will be analysed as aesthetic narratives.

The way in which the reader sees Nature is very important, especially when it comes to the way of interpretation. Moreover, the way one sees Nature (for instance, a character in a literary text) can help the reader to understand, when it comes to the definition of the relation between Nature and the human beings. The questions may have different answers - for example, do we depend on Nature? Are we using Nature? Is it possible to understand Nature itself as an entity, in a way in which Nature can have a real dialectic fusion with the human beings? Or, is it possible to claim that Nature and the human beings are actually each other's reflections, exactly as the reader can see in some selected literary texts, when it comes to define the relation between Nature and so-called human nature? In this research, I aim to answer these questions through three parts of analysis, as follows.

***

In Anthony Doerr's short story, *The Hunter's Wife*, in *The Shell Collector: Stories*, there is a description which shows Nature under the sharp observation of the hunter himself. Nature does exist. But not only that: Nature itself, indeed, is depending on the delicate balance between Nature itself and the human beings. As the hunter claims, the order of Nature makes the contradictions to the cities, because

> [t]here is no order in that world, [...]. But here [in Nature]

> there is. Here I can see things I'd never see down there, things most folks are blind to. With no great reach of imagination [the hunter's wife] could see him fifty years hence, still lacing his boots, still gathering his rifle, all the world to see and him dying happy having seen only this valley (Doerr 55).

According to the hunter's way of seeing Nature and his verbal description to his wife in this quotation, the reader can come to an understanding, which shows that there are two, at least to the hunter himself, very different worlds - 'that world' as referring to the cities of the human beings, and 'here' as referring to the hills and Nature.

Both worlds come to represent two separate, and yet, not totally irrelevant senses of order. On the one hand, the order of Nature can be seen, can be heard, and can be felt by the hunter, as 'huge saucers of ice' comes to melt (Doerr 53). On the other hand, the relation between Nature and the human beings does depend on one's recognition and interpretation, as the 'sound of water running' feels like an urge in the hunter's 'soul' (Doerr 53).

Once again, through the hunter's interpretive words, the reader can see that Nature has an order that cannot be cheated or be fooled by the human beings. In Nature, what one can see is what one can get. It is exactly like the hunter himself has experienced, as the reader can see in the literary text. When the hunter sees that 'trout were rising through the chill brown water to take the first insects' (Doerr 53), he feels that it is the season of Spring.

Moreover, in the hunter's dreams, he can see wolves. And yet, ironically, as no one sees any single wolf in the hills, at least for 'twenty years' (Doerr 65). The unbalanced ecosystem makes the wolves unseen by the human beings. For the hunter, wolves represent the primary desire of being alive and keep hunting in

Nature, because wolves are not domestic animals which can be kept by the human beings in an urban space - such as in a 'zoo', waiting for their 'visitors' (Berger 23). Wolves also do not need to depend on some kind of owners, as they were originally born to live in the wilderness and to be able to survive in their own living environment.

As Sigmund Freud points out in his *The Interpretation of Dreams*, as the reader can see from this point, that the hunter's dreams are revealing his unconscious desire as a 'psychological significance' (Freud 595), as the unseen wolves are visualised in the hunter's dreams. In this respect, as Freud terms it, a dream can represent one's unconscious desire, just as the reader can see in the case of the hunter. That is the reason why having a dream can be seen as a sort of wish-fulfilment, in a way in which the viewer is having hope.

According to the hunter, the cities, on the other hand, when comparing to the hills, have 'no order' (Doerr 55). This world of cities, having 'no order', is actually referring to the world of the human beings. In this world of 'no order', in some ways, the rhythm of Nature can be used and can be manipulated by the human beings, for all different kinds of purposes. For example, as the 'client' (Doerr 54) of the hunter comes to show the reader, the world of the cities is a combination of various human desires. The hunter needs to apply this world of no order to Nature, in order to satisfy his clients, as they 'wanted to see grizzlies, track a wolverine, even shoot sandhill cranes' (Doerr 54).

Those people, as the hunter's clients, come from the cities - they do want to conquer Nature to satisfy their own needs, and do want to keep it indoor. For example, as the hunter recalls that 'they wanted the heads of seven-by-seven royal bulls for their dens' (Doerr 54), sometimes even just for the sake of a style of decoration. In some ways, the phrase 'no order' (Doerr 55) can refer to a situation of being 'stupid' (Doerr 54), when '[a] bloodthirsty New Yorker claimed only to want to photograph black bears, then pulled a pistol from his boot and fired wildly at two cubs and their mother' (Doerr 54). The cities have no order - just like the human beings who are behaving in some irrational ways. When those people are in Nature, coming from the cities, their irrationality become something very 'stupid', as their behaviours are the key cause of this unbalanced situation of Nature and human habitations.

***

Nature and the cities are two different orders, as the reader can see from the above examples from Doerr's short story, *The Hunter's Wife*. Moreover, the reader can also understand Nature and the cities in the way in which these two orders can represent - especially through narratives forms, verbal and visual arts - a sort of metaphor, which is full of 'semantic codes' (Grace 194) of the urban and the rural spaces. For example, in Edith Wharton's novel, *Summer*, the reader can see that Nature is depicted in a way in which human emotions can be released and be understood. In other words, the 'pleasure of feeling' (Wharton, *Summer* 13) does not come from cultural events in the cities, or houses and rooms, or library and books. Rather, in the 'wilderness' (Wharton, *Summer* 14), the main female character Charity Royall can feel herself free from the external world.

Charity Royall, although works in a library, she does not want to 'be bothered about books' (Wharton, *Summer* 13). Her attitude does set up an opposition between urban and rural codes, as if the cities and all kinds of cultural events make her feel the 'superiority' (Wharton, *Summer* 13) of male domination. As a woman, although without too much proper education, she does have her own feelings and emotions, just like a human being. However, at home, she feels like she is some kind of property of Mr. Royall's. As a woman, Charity is depending on this well-respected lawyer in the small town - no matter she likes it or not. Comparing to the wilderness, the house she lives in is only a 'sad house' (Wharton, *Summer* 15), as Mr. Royall and Charity sit face to face. With him, ironically, she does feel 'the depths of isolation', because she does not have 'no particular affection for him' (Wharton, *Summer* 15).

In Edith Wharton's another rather famous novel, *The Age of Innocence*, there are also signs of this urban / rural dualism. This time, the male main character Newland Archer is thinking about escaping from all kinds of duties in a way in which an urban space such as New York City comes to represent. The place itself is not a real kind of wilderness,

> [b]ut Newport represented the escape from duty into an atmosphere of unmitigated holiday-making. Archer had tried to persuade May to spend the summer on a remote island off the coast of Maine (called, appropriately enough, Mount Desert), where a few hardy Bostonians and Philadelphians were camping in 'native' cottages, and whence came reports of enchanting scenery and a wild, almost trapper like existence amid woods and waters (Wharton, *Innocence* 167).

Unlike any other kinds of opposition, Newland's (and also including the upper-middle class New Yorkers') sense of opposition between Nature and the cities is created by the urban dwellers. In other words, Nature is a kind of sense, which is designed and is prepared for those people to escape from the cities and all codes - culture, business, duty, so on and so forth.

The city dwellers - wealthy ones especially - particularly go to the island (the created Nature), to do camping, in order to feel free and not to be stressful. Even they do not go to the island, they can still dress up and go to the park, to have a nice day out.

For example, as the viewer can see in two paintings - Maurice Brazil Prendergast's painting, *Mothers and Children in the Park* (Dwight 26), and William Merritt Chase's painting, *Lilliputian Boat Lake, Central Park* (Dwight 28) - there are quite a lot of 'social events' going on in those people's leisure time, including 'teas, picnics, dinners, and dances as well as sports like yachting, tennis, golf, and polo' (Dwight 29). Wealthy New Yorkers, if they do not go abroad to seek inspirations in Paris or in London, staying in some kind of artificial Natural-like environment in the city can also relieve them from a sort of daily routine, at some point.

***

In some other cases, as the reader can see in different literary texts, Nature does help the human beings to see everything in a comparative way, as both orders - Nature's and the human beings', would show an interaction. For example, when a person is feeling confused, he or she may turn to Nature for help through a form of interaction between human labour and the earth. In the Turkish writer Orhan Pamuk's recent novel, *The Red-haired Woman*, the reader can see that when the narrator comes to learn and to practice the technique of well-digging, he realises that if one can speak the language of the soil, one may have a better chance to survive. The best way to explain this is to read through the narrator, Mr. Cem's revelation,

> [f]or earth was made up of many layers, just like the celestial sphere, which had seven. [...]. Two meters of rich black earth might conceal a loamy, impermeable, bone-dry layer of wretched soil or sand under-neath. To work out where to dig for water as they paced the ground, the old masters had to decipher the language of the soil, of the grass, insects, and birds, and detect the signs of rock or clay

underfoot (Pamuk 17).

The language of soil is symbolic enough to come to the rescue, if the human beings have sufficient 'skills' (Pamuk 17) to decode the signs which are already in Nature. This process of decoding the message of Nature requires, apart from other 'skills' of well-digging, a sort of listening skill - involving a sort of full concentration - in a way which is very much like the 'doctor putting his ear to 'a sick baby's chest' (Pamuk 17). Nature, in this literary text, does come to help with desperate human conditions, in a way which the human beings look for the order of Nature and try to learn and to master it, for the sake of survival.

Also, the reader can see more other examples in different literary texts when Nature comes to reveal human emotions. It feels so real and vivid, as if one can almost understand and can almost identify Nature as a part of human nature. This way does help the reader to see what is going on in a character's mind. For instance, in William Shakespeare's famous tragic play, *King Lear*, the old King, in M. C. Bradbrook's reading, among the scholars, comes to arouse the reader's attention. The reader pays attention to the old King's emotions, because he or she can sympathise the King when reading the literary text, when the

King 'kneels to pray for the "poor naked wretches" who are out in the storm' (Bradbrook 92). In this case, the term Nature (as the storm in which the King is situated in), as Marilyn French points out, 'means *natura* and also *human nature*; at times it refers to physical, at times to psychological dimensions of a human (French 244).

And yet, the relation between Nature and the human society is indeed, the key point for the reader to notice. It is simply because this relation is not necessarily always smooth, or it is not often very easy to understand, as it may seem to be. For example, in Terry Eagleton's book chapter *'Wuthering Heights'*, he argues that

> Nature, in any case, is no true 'outside' to society, since its conflicts are transposed into the social arena. In one sense the novel [*Wuthering Heights*] sharply contrasts Nature and society; in another sense it grasps civilised life as a higher distillation of ferocious natural appetite. Nature, then, is a thoroughly ambiguous category, inside and outside society simultaneously (Eagleton 58).

For Eagleton, as the reader can see in the above quotation,

Nature in Emily Brontë's novel *Weathering Height* cannot be simply read or be easily reduced as a background. Rather, Nature comes to play a significant role, in a way in which human nature can be seen through the characters and the societies where they are situated in. The society, in this novel, according to Eagleton, reveals critical issues which can be read in several 'symptomatic' (Eagleton 59) ways, as the characters Heathcliff and his lover Catherine come to show the reader in the literary text.

According to Margaret Homans, the reader can understand that 'Nature, or the literal as it is represented by nature, appears to provoke a sort of 'attitude' and a 'strategy of writing' (Homans

18-19) in Emily Brontë's *Weathering Height*. Homans's claim comes closer to Eagleton's, showing to the reader once again, the ambiguity of the relation between Nature and the human society. For example, Cathy's repression of 'the Heathcliff-nature complex' (Homan 18) and Cathy's 'madness' (Homan 19) come to suggest and to indicate this ambiguity. Both Homans and Eagleton suggest that this 'symptomatic' (Eagleton 59) way of reading can show the reader a contrast between 'the wild energy of the Heights' (McKibben 162) and the 'true natures' (McKibben 169) of the characters - especially the young couple - Catherine and Hareton who are into books, reading, culture and education. Nature seems to be mild and welcoming, as the reader can understand, when human nature comes to bring out its best part through education. Carmen Perez Riu also points out that 'the withdrawal of the opportunity to become educated is presented as one of the most cruel forms of oppression for both Heathcliff and Hareton' (Riu 167). Nature is not rough and untamed, when the human beings are well-educated. Nature can be symbolically referred to some human conditions, especially the profound human nature in this gothic novel.

The textual world of Emily Brontë does have an implication that culture as a sort of 'refuge from or reflex of material conditions' (Eagleton 59). Comparing to Nature, culture itself does bring a different energy in the society. For example, Cathy's five weeks away from her home totally make a difference - as if she becomes a new well-educated person - not as the old wild Cathy anymore. After coming back from Thrushcross Grange, the 'reform' shows that Cathy's 'self-respect' is raised

> with fine clothes and flattery, [...], so that, instead of a wild, hatless little savage jumping into the house, [...], there lighted from a handsome black pony a very dignified person, with brown ringlets falling from the cover of a

> feathered beaver, and a long cloth habit, which she was obliged to hold up with both hands that she might sail in (Brontë 57).

It is a true dialectical moment between Nature and Culture when the reader can read Nature in a way in which it comes to represent a character's inner self in a symbolic way. Cultivated, losing her wild energy, and taking the manner of language (such as 'flattery'), Cathy seems to be changed, at least through the appearance and the behaviour as the reader can see. Although in the same Nature, she is different now from her friend Heathcliff.

Comparing to her, without any culture, he is only a 'dirty boy' with 'his thick, uncombed hair' (Brontë 57).

***

Nature has a power of healing. The reader can see this point much clearer when the character in the literary text has confusions or troubles with human relations. For example, in Anthony Doerr's short story, *The Caretaker*, the reader can see that the main character Joseph Saleeby

> spends most of his time squatting on the front step

> watching his mother tend her garden. Her fingers pry weeds from the soil or cull spent vines or harvest snap beans, the beans plunking regularly into a metal bowl, and he listens to her diatribes on the hardships of war, the importance of maintaining a structured lifestyle. "We cannot stop living because of conflict, Joseph," she says. "We must persevere." (Doerr 131).

Joseph's mother insists that a certain way of living is the key to keep things going. The rhythm of life may be disturbed because of difficulties in all kinds of human relations - personal, national, international, so on and so forth. And yet, this rhythm - this ‘style’, as Joseph’s mother terms it - has to be maintained and to be managed, so that one will not lose this culture, this way of life, as a human being.

Joseph himself cannot see or cannot understand the meaning of his mother’s words - ‘we must persevere’ - as his mother, ‘each morning’, ‘makes him read a column of the English dictionary, selected at random, before he is allowed to set foot outside’ (Doerr 130), until later when he is forced to escape from his ‘small collapsing house in the hills outside Monrovia in Liberia’ (Doerr 130), to go to the United States and try to start a new way of living.

In Astoria, Oregon of the United States, Joseph is hired to tend '*Ocean Meadows, a ninety-acre estate, orchard and home*' (Doerr 137). And yet, his awakening will be coming until he tries to build up and to tend his own secret garden. It seems that working with Nature can cure him, step by step. Joseph 'chooses a plot on a hill, concealed by the forest, overlooking the western edge of the main house and a slice of the lawn' of Mr. Twyman's (Doerr 141 - 142). During the process, he can try to forgive and to forget, in order to keep living his live, as 'he is remaking an order, a structure to his hours. It feels good, tending the soil, hauling water. It feels healthy' (Doerr 152).

On the other hand, a photographic image about Nature can also have the power of healing. Even when a character does not work with Nature directly, as Joseph and his mother do, one can still feel this power of healing through a work of art. In Anthony Doerr's short story, *Mkondo*, the female main character Naima, the reader can see that she, like an artist, who can create an interactive space through the photographic image between Nature and the human beings.

Naima's first photo makes her feel alive again, in Ohio. For taking that photo, she was waiting for the clouds, when they ‘parted gently, a thin ray of light nudged through, illuminating the oak, and she made her exposure’ (Doerr 207). This natural sunlight seems to be a message from God, guiding her way of finding her joy of life again. Seeing the photographic image - ‘oak branches bloomed over with sun, a fracture in the haze beyond’ (Doerr 207) - Naima finds her own ‘oldest feeling’ (Doerr 207) of being alive. Taking the photo of a scene in Nature, and looking at that photo, for Naima, it feels like ‘a darkness tear away from her eyes’ (Doerr 207), so that she can see the world again - ‘for the first time’ (Doerr 207) in a very long time.

***

Is here a true dialectical moment between the human beings and Nature? How can the reader see this dialectical moment? The answer, in some ways, can be found especially in one of Virginia Woolf's writings - her novel *To the Lighthouse*. Woolf depicts 'a central element of the landscape and of the formal design'. This idea comes from her childhood memories of the Summer holidays in Cornwall (Fleishman 606). I would argue, in Woolf's novel *To the Lighthouse,* there is a particular moment of 'intimacy' (Woolf 187), in a way in which Lily and Mrs.

Ramsay are sitting together in Nature - to be precise - 'on the beach' (Woolf 186).

Sitting side by side, in Nature and in silence, these two women are having a moment of communication - with each other and with Nature through observing what they see in Nature. Their observations come to reveal some significant meanings, at first, through looking at a work of art and then asking about it:

> 'Is it a boat? Is it a cork?' [Mrs Ramsay] would say, Lily repeated, turning back, [...], to her canvas. Heaven be praised for it, the problem of space remained, she thought,

> taking up her brush again. It glared at her. The whole mass of the picture was poised upon that weight. Beautiful and bright it should be on the surface, feathery and evanescent, one colour melting into another like the colours on a butterfly's wing; but beneath the fabric must be clamped together with bolts of iron (Woolf 186).

Giving shapes, lines, and colours, Lily's canvas (which is a work-in-progress painting) comes to show the way in which she understands what she sees in Nature. This understanding comes to show the reader the dialectical moment of the artist and

Nature. In Lily's eyes, Nature is firstly internalised, and secondly externalised, through a form of fine arts.

In silence, as the canvas seems to gaze back at Lily, Mrs. Ramsay also seems to try to guess what she can see in Lily's canvas (a boat, or a cork). On the surface, everything seems to be 'uncommunicative' (Woolf 187), as no one says anything verbally, or through any language. These two women are only sitting 'in silence' (Woolf 187). And yet, there is a delicate sensation of this moment, if not verbally but visually - it is something sacred which can be felt by the two characters in the literary text. They are both women - one gives birth to her children in her family, as another woman gives birth to her works of art.

For Lily, at this very moment of 'squeezing her tube of green paint' (Woolf 187), language or any kinds of verbal expression is somehow not sufficient enough. In order to express this sensation of hers, which comes from the moment sitting with Mrs. Ramsay in Nature, Lily chooses to stick to her painting. This emotion and this sensation are, in a way, 'extraordinarily fertile' (Woolf 187), which makes her unconsciously do 'a little hole in the sand and covered it up' (Woolf 187). This gesture of Lily's is also having a symbolic meaning. Just like the sea turtles, after laying their eggs, they also cover up the holes, to protect their eggs. This gesture is symbolically meaningful, in order to let the reader know that Lily feels that her great idea for her artistic creation is born.

As a researcher, my concern here, of course, is not to ask how real Lily's canvas can come to represent Nature, as some people may keep asking about how real a viewer can see in her boat or in her lighthouse. Moreover, it is also not my ultimate goal to identify the content of her painting - questions such as who and what - they do not refer to the messages that Virginia Woolf is trying to give to her readers. For example, if one did that, eventually, one would be trapped into the look and the appearance of works of art and Nature. It means that we will always see works of art as a copy of Nature, in a way in which works of art can never be seen as good as Nature. In a comparative manner, both works of art and Nature have meanings - if any - it is all because of a concern of humanity. As the character Polixenes in William Shakespeare's *The Winter's Tale* comes to remind the reader that 'in defence of art' -

> Yet Nature is made better by no mean
>
> But Nature makes that mean; so over that art

> Which you say adds to Nature, is an art
>
> That Nature makes, [...].
>
> (IV. iv. 89 - 92, qtd. Shakespeare 1566).

The point here in this quotation is, as long as Nature comes to inspire the human beings, one shall do as what the artists do, in order to try to express one's thoughts and feels in artistic creations. Works of art can be seen, in this way, as an outcome of the freedom of expression, in a way in which it is creating new artistic forms which inspire by looking at Nature and by recognising its existence, as Nature itself is a very significant element. Nature shows the reader that it is really possible to achieve an artistic vision of one's own. As the reader can see, Lily achieves her own artistic vision, in the end of *To the Lighthouse*, when her canvas externalises Nature in a form of fine arts.

***

The French Surrealist Louis Aragon, in his novel *Paris Peasant*, points out that the human beings cannot appreciate Nature as it is (for example, people always want to understand things in a more scientific way, without any human emotions, as ‘light is a vibration’). Or, one cannot see the importance of Nature in one’s life, because he or she comes to a point that everything has to be rational, instead of emotional, as one’s ‘stupid rationalism contains an unimaginably large element of materialism. This fear of error which everything recalls to me at every moment of the flight of my ideas, this mania for control, makes man prefer reason’s imagination to the imagination of the senses’ (Aragon 9).

If the reader considers all kinds of literary texts as a form of fine arts in verbal representations, it is not impossible for one to understand that this art of narrative - if it can be any authentic at all - can actually show the human beings the way in which it expresses this exploration of the senses of human. In terms of artistic creations, for an artist, it is important to have 'the imagination of the senses', as Aragon terms it. In order to see the profound human nature, an artist does need to have true fusions with Nature, in his or in her vision.

2

The Reading Self

The reading self is a reader. The text can be literary ones or, in symbolic ways, a person, a city, a painting, a photograph, so on and so forth - as long as one reads. Apart from being an author, or being a reader, the self, eventually, is a human. Most of the time, when we think about Marcel Proust's *À la Recherche du temps perdu*, or when we read about someone's reading about Proust's work, we learn a rather common idea that 'his tasting a Madeleine soaked in tea' (Shore 237) is a representation of a 'physical sensation' (Shore 237), using in his text as 'a moment of vision' (Shore 232) when memories come back to the present self, constituting a moment in which the past and the present become one.

Marcel Proust, in the readers' eyes, is an author, who has been remembered in a particular literary style that he created. But it is exactly because of this, we somehow tend to forget about this - before Marcel Proust the author, there is Marcel Proust the person. He is a real human being who lived a life. That famous Madeleine cake connects to another real person in Proust's life - a family member who baked the cake - his grandmother. Before, or, after soaked ourselves in the labyrinth of Proust's texts, we ought to remind ourselves that the cake itself is not only a word, or only something literary in any case. Its taste does mean something extremely special to a person, in his childhood. As a writer and an adult, Proust recalled the memory which related to this cake - suddenly, automatically, and vividly.

Reading words and literary texts by writers, philosophers, or critics, we, as readers, firstly have a feeling of respecting these people, aroused by reading their work. We are fully amazed by what we read, because those literary texts stimulate our imagination, making us learn something new, feel something new, as we are all one step closer to be better persons. And yet, interestingly, all great writers or philosophers or critics - they tend to start reading when they were children. There are also, some family members - such as grandmothers of the authors who help to develop this interest of reading.

***

Walter Benjamin, in his *Berlin Childhood around 1900*,

mentioned about the way in which he came to his grandmother's apartment - Blumeshof 12 - feeling very safe and comfortable. He read his grandmother's handwriting, looked at her furniture, as a little boy. Moreover, in the grandmother's apartment, there was also the sensation of the sound of the doorbell ringing - as '[n]o bell sounded friendlier' (Benjamin 86).

As a boy, Benjamin felt even 'safer' in his grandmothers, comparing to be in his parents' (Benjamin 86). It is exactly this feeling of being safe, he could let his imagination go as far as it could be. Firstly, Benjamin read through the postcards that his grandmother sent him, during her 'long sea voyages' (Benjamin

86). All those places and all the high-class residences showed his grandmother's spirit of being a part of 'cosmopolitan' (Benjamin 86). For Benjamin the little boy - not the famous German critic, writer, and philosopher - his grandmother's handwriting showed that 'these places as so entirely occupied by her' (Benjamin 87) - as if his grandmother was the Queen, and these places 'became colonies of Blumeshof' (Benjamin 87) in this little boy's imagination.

Reading does stimulate one's imagination - no matter for a child or an adult. And this power of imagination can help one to achieve something particular. Benjamin's postcards, and his reading of them, later were developed into different energies. The reading became his passion of collecting (such as postcards). He also observed material objects in the cities (such as toys, children's books, Paris, Moscow) and paid attention to other kinds of collectors (such as the rag picking motive in Baudelaire's writing).

With these energies (just a little start of reading - how amazing!), Benjamin put his literary efforts in, starting with little travel scenes in the form of 'a private travel journal' (Benjamin, *Archive* 172) when he was eighteen. Later on, from 1924, Benjamin's travel writings can be read and be understood as many symbolic postcards in words from different places - Paris, Moscow, Marseille, Naples, so on and so forth. Each writing is 'a memento' (Benjamin, *Archive* 172), in a way in which Benjamin expressed his dreams and desires in his verbal postcards.

***

This is an example, from a collection of Benjamin's archives, one of his verbal postcards. It is in a form of a personal notes taking. And yet, for a reader like me, it feels very poetic, in a way which this travel scene can be read as a poem:

Ibizan Sequence

Revolution and festival

Distance and images

Sovier dream

Once is as good as never

Attempt to give everything in life a consequence

Proust note

Memories

Roulette

Narrative and healing

Style of recollections

(Benjamin, *Archive* 170).

***

Again, Benjamin's 'bourgeois security' does not only come from words or readings. More importantly, it comes from the material condition of his grandmother's apartment - in a way in which mainly is represented by the furniture. In the little boy's eyes, Benjamin's grandmother owned 'a type of furniture that, having capriciously incopporated styles of ornament from different centuries' (Benjamin 88), showing 'its own duration' (Benjamin 88) of timelessness.

Later on, this meditation of material conditions, coming from a childhood memory, will be developed by Walter Benjamin the critic, writer and philosopher, in a way in which the dream images of commodity will be recognised as the myth of modernity, as the city itself becomes a representation of the 'dream-world' (Gilloch 119). Because of his father's mother, Benjamin had an initial image of a city (Berlin), as if it was a dream, under a sort of spell, as 'the street became [...] a realm inhabited by shades of immortal yet departed grandmothers'

(Benjamin 89).

***

The point of calling the reader's attention to Benjamin's childhood, his relation to his grandmother and her apartment, and his experience of reading - all is to show the similarities of some other boys' childhood backgrounds, for example, such as Jean-Paul Sartre's and Orhan Pamuk's. In these two writers' childhood memories, the reader can see the way in which the reading self, the family member (the boy's grandmother), and the material objects such as books - are strongly connected.

In Sartre's autobiographical writing, *Words*, he showed a vivid image, which is about a little boy's observation to his reading environment - the house of his grandfather and grandmother. Most importantly, the house was not just full of books - people who lived in the house were also passionate readers of those books.

The books in Sartre's grandparents' house were like 'ancient monuments which had witnessed' birth (Sartre 28). The image of birth comes to refer not only to a physical level, as seeing a baby was born. Rather, those books represented the intellectual birth of Sartre himself as a little boy, who was attracted by the appearance and the physical condition of the books.

As Sartre remembered, in his gradfather's study, books were 'everywhere'. Moreover,

> it was forbidden to dust them except once a year, before the October term. Even before I could read, I already revered these raised stones; upright or leaning, wedged together like bricks on the library shelves or nobly spaced like avenues of dolmens, I felt that our family prosperity depended on them (Sartre 28).

Even before he started reading a book, Sartre already knew that these books refer to 'a future as calm as [his] past' (Sartre 28). He even 'touched them' (Sartre 28) when no one was around, just to feel the dust of the books, in order to 'honour' (Sartre 28) his hands - as if these books in his grandfather's study were sacred objects, and he was worshipping them in his own very private 'ceremonies' (Sartre 28).

As a boy, Sartre also observed the way in which his grandparent read books. His grandfather, for example, opens a volume 'at the right page' (Sartre 28). In *Words,* Sartre used the image of food to depict books in his grandfather's house. Books were like ‘oysters’ (Sartre 28) and their pages were like their ‘internal organs’ (Sartre 28) - which were very tasty.

The books were like spiritual food for the soul of Sartre’s grandfather; the intellectual food for his brain. On the other hand, Sartre’s grandmother, used to read her books which were borrowed from the local library ‘with pleasure’ (Sartre 29). The feeling of joy could be recognised from her lips - a mysterious smile - as the one Sartre saw later on Leonardo da Vinci’s painting - ‘on the lips of the Mona Lisa’ (Sartre 29). The grandmother’s remark of the art of ‘read between the lines’ (Sartre 29), and also her smile, in some ways, make the reader see the connection between reading, childhood memory, and works of art.

***

In Orhan Pamuk's *Istanbul: Memories of a City*, he mentioned about a very similar experience, which is very much like Walter Benjamin's. It was about reading in his grandmother's house. For Pamuk, it was 'a short period before beginning school, when it had been decided that it was time [he] learned to read' (Pamuk 106).

Pamuk, as a little boy, did not only learn 'the mystery of

the alphabet' (Pamuk 106), but also identified himself with his grandmother's 'Pamuk Apartments' (Pamuk 108). Every object in Pamuk Apartments was having an image of Orhan, and his grandmother as the way he knew her: the visual objects (bed, mirror, bags, newspapers, pillows); and the smells: a mixture of soap, cologne, dust, and wood (Pamuk 108).

There was a dressing table 'with a winged mirror' (Pamuk 107), which was much more vivid in his memory than anything else, because Pamuk used to 'lose [himself] in the reflections' (Pamuk 107). The mirror did not only unify one's own image as a self, in a Lacanian way. It also created an authentic image of his grandmother,

> who spent half the day in bed, and never made herself up, had positioned the table in such a way that she could see all the way down the long corridor, past the service entrance, the vestibule and right across the sitting room to the windows that looked out to the street, thus allowing her to supervise everything happening in the house - the comings and goings, the conversations in corners and the quarrelling grandchildren beyond - without getting out of bed (Pamuk 107).

Apart from the mirror and the image and naming her grandchildren 'after a victorious Sultan' (Pamuk 109), Pamuk's grandmother also had a 'slim leather-bound notebook' (Pamuk 108) which showed her interest in 'official etiquette' (Pamuk 109). In her notebook, Pamuk's grandmother 'recorded bills, memories, meals, expenses, plans, and meteorological developments' (Pamuk 108)- all these made the notebook look like an Ottoman protocol book.

Reading something to Orhan from her notebook, the grandmother would give him 'a strange, mocking smile' (Pamuk

109). As a reader of Pamuk's text and a viewer of Leonardo da Vinci's *Mona Lisa*, I somehow wonder - is that a smile to her own condition? Or, that strange smile just reflected the nonsensical life itself, so that we all ought to have some sense of humour?

***

There is a part worth quoting, in the beginning of Chapter 14 *Swann's Essay*, in Anthony Bailey's biography *A View of Delft: Vermeer Then and Now*. The relation among art, life, looking, reading and writing is somehow inter-connected. When we look at a work of art, we can feel that

> [g]reat art raises the question: is this the real point of things, to make constructs of this kind? Vermeer's art especially puts the question almost as an ultimatum: What in life is more important than these abstractions of life, these dreams modelled in paint that are slightly offset from 'reality'? (Bailey 243).

The sensation of reading a verbal art such as a literary work, comparing to the sensation of looking at a visual art such as a painting, we may say that there are different sensations. And yet, as a viewer of a painting, or, as a reader of a book, one can feel that the function of looking, or the function of reading is for one to realise one's own solitude.

When we read a page of a book, or when we look at a painting, we feel that we are naked. It is because of the act of reading or the act of looking, at that very moment, we are immediately out of the material world where we are in. We are with ourselves - either an emotion, or a memory, or an inner being which represents our own thoughts, when we are looking or when we are reading.

***

In Virginia Woolf's *Women and Writing*, we can see the way in which Woolf, as a writer, was inspired by other writers, through her reading of other writers' work. To be able to write, most of the time, it does mean that one is able to read enough. This happens to many writers, including Jean-Paul Sartre. For example, Sartre started writing poetry, simply because of his reading of his grandfather Charles Schweitzer's letter.

During the Summer holiday, as a boy of eight or night of age, Sartre 'received a poem' (Sartre, *Words* 89) from his grandfather. Sartre wrote a reply 'with a poem' (Sartre, *Words* 89). Reading and writing between the grandfather and the grandson became a habit. This letter writing, receiving, and writing back - in a way - highlights 'a new link' (Sartre, *Words* 89) between these two men, because they wrote 'in a language forbidden to women' (Sartre, *Words* 89).

The language of literature (not French language in particular), at least in Sartre's boyhood understanding, belongs to Literary Men, not women (even they were dear family members such as Sartre's sisters, Louise and Anne-Marie). As a man, Sartre was somehow consciously enough to enjoy literature, reading and writing as if he was playing a game - 'for its own sake: an only son' (Sartre, *Words* 91).

This literary game, to Sartre, was very much fun, not only because he 'could play it alone' (Sartre, *Words* 91), but also he could feel that he was '*a writer*' (Sartre, *Words* 91). All activities were seen as 'one more monkey-trick' (Sartre, *Words* 92) to him - such as 'to blend memory and imagination' (Sartre, *Words* 91), changing the 'description' (Sartre, *Words* 91) of some places in Jules Verne's novels, or making the plots 'a complex' by blending 'a wide variety of incident, pouring everything' (Sartre, *Words* 93) together from all kinds of readings.

***

Virginia Woolf, on the other hand, shows us the difficulties of making literature a women's language. Apart from using men's names (like the Brontës did) for publication, or just putting 'The Author' instead of using a name (like Jane Austen or Mary Shelly), a woman's relation to writing is much more complicated - not only because a woman cannot be recognised as a writer, but also, a woman cannot master a language of literature, which belongs to men.

Female writers and their female characters do not only refer to a simple relation between reading and writing - or a simple blending of memory and imagination. In Woolf's writing, as one can see and as one can feel in her words - female writers and female characters are true representations of 'womanhood' (Woolf, *Women and Writing* 67). For the female writers, especially, writing is in some ways, 'the first painful step on the road to freedom' (Woolf, *Women and Writing* 67) - for the sake of discovering the real meaning of being a woman.

***

A woman, as a writer, her point of view and her observation

can be very much different than a man's. And yet, even so, a woman cannot feel powerful unless she is able to use a language of her own, to have her own voice. For example, again in *Women and Writing*, Woolf also explained the way in which women have troubles to express themselves because of the use of language, as

> the women of the middle class has now some leisure, some education, and some liberty to investigate the world in which she lives, it will not be in this generation or in the next that she will have adjusted her position or given a clear account of her powers. 'I have the feelings of a woman,'

> says Bathsheba in *Far from the Madding Crowd,* 'but I have only the language of men' (Woolf, *Women and Writing* 67).

Is it really possible to have a sort of - a woman's language? For sure, a woman would be able to have a room - so that she could write, as Woolf urged in her *A Room of One's Own.* Isn't it really, in the end, would all come down to the style of expression, which comes to determine whose language is: his or hers?

A language is used by people and their milieu. And yet, it is also continuously reshaping and transforming itself, as the condition (people and their milieu) change. It is unthinkable to say that a woman's literary productions are all within the frame of the patriarchy. A woman is not a copy of a man's language, of a man's education, of a man's leisure, of a man's so on and so forth.

***

In *Orlando* and in *Swann's Way*, one can see that both Virginia Woolf and Marcel Proust use a work of art to depict the emotions of love of the central characters - Orlando and Swann. In his book *Painting and the Novel*, Jeffrey Meyers mentioned about several paintings of Vermeer's, in a way in which Proust's characters - particularly Marcel and Swann - have a complex relation with their lovers and their lives.

Meyers also pointed out that Proust's own appreciation to Vermeer's *View of Delft*, that touching and heart-warming 'patch of yellow' (Meyers 115) is, indeed, a symbol of 'a harmony' - as the painting itself is 'undramatic, passionless, remote and detached' and 'perfect' - which comes to be 'an absolute contrast to the mutability of Proust's world' (Meyers 115). Proust's textual world is full of emotional ups and downs, love, hate, passion, and jealousy. The heart-warming yellow is just a perfect contrast.

In Woolf's *Orlando*, there is a painting looks more like an inspiration to the whole love scene of Orlando and Sasha, which will lead to Orlando's solitude. Woolf did not mention the name of the painter, or the title of the painting. The reader can only know that the painting which Orlando is looking at is 'a Dutch snow scene by an unknown artist' (Woolf 69 - 70).

Lovers, ice skating, escaping from the crowd, and from a frozen river: all these are elements which construct the love scene of Orlando and Sasha. I find that Hendrick Avercamp's painting, *Winter Landscape with a Frozen River and Figures* (Hall 27), can somehow help the readers to visualise this love scene in *Orlando*.

From the text, we can see that Sasha wanted to be away from 'the crowd of common people', because '[in] Russia they had rivers ten miles broad on which one could gallop six horses abreast all day long without meeting a soul' (Woolf 42). She wanted to be alone with Orlando, to have some privacy.

Woolf did not describe the frozen Thames in detail - not as what we see in Avercamp's painting. And yet, the painting shows 'the receding banks, with flag-bedecked booths on the right and a dyke on the left - leading the eye towards a distant town and a sizeable ship, frozen in the ice' (Hall 26). The crowd in the painting reveals a 'cheerful' (Hall 26) atmosphere, as the viewers can also see 'worldly booths for refreshments and entertainment' (Hall 26). The young couple 'arm in arm, occur in a drawing in the Royal Collection at Windsor' (Hall 26). Imagining, as if among them, there were Orlando and Sasha, on their way to be with each other 'in privacy all day long where there were none to marvel or to stare' (Woolf 42).

After Sasha left, Orlando's solitude indicated the meaning of the act of reading and the self. The reading of books and the looking of a painting - the same solitude we can find when we think about Proust's Swann - especially 'at the end of his affair with Odette, when Swann discovers she was not in his *style*, his essay on Vermeer replaces Odette in his life' (Meyers 117). Swann wants to return to The Hague, to see Vermeer's paintings again - to be away from where Odette is.

Orlando, on the other hand, wants to read, in order to be alone. In reading, he can feel his passion as 'a nobleman' (Woolf 71) who loves literature. The habit of reading also has a trace of his childhood. Orlando, '[a]s a child, he was sometimes found at midnight by a page still reading' (Woolf 71). It is because he knew that reading can 'substitute a phantom for reality' (Woolf 71). When he opens a book, he reads as if he was a 'naked man'

(Woolf 72). He sees nothing between himself and the page he is reading. He gives his whole heart and soul to what he is reading.

At that very moment of his 'solitude' (Woolf 66), every worldly material seems to be 'invisible' or 'disappeared' or 'vanished' (Woolf 72) - 'plate, linen, houses, men-servants, carpets' (Woolf 71). He can truly be alone, to forget his reality.

Great readers are not all great writers. But great writers are definitely all great readers. In 'How should one read a book', the reader can see that Virginia Woolf's strategy of reading is very helpful. First of all, a reader will need to see 'the shape' of a book - is it 'a barn', 'a pig-sty', 'or a cathedral' (Woolf, *The*

Common Reader II 267). Once a reader recognises the book as a whole - namely, the main idea, the developing points - after that, a reader will be able to move on to the second stage of reading - to be able to make sense of the reading with his or her own criticism, as to have a reader's own 'visionary shape' (Woolf, *The Common Reader II* 267) of a book - analysis, interpretation, criticism, reflection, so on and so forth.

The first stage is the most difficult, because the reader needs to get involved in 'the true complexity of reading' (Woolf, *Common Reader II* 267). It is not a direct process - in a way in which a book is identified as its own true shape. In other words, according to Woolf, it is very hard to get the first impression right. And yet, if a reader wants to take all in and to see the true shape of a book, he or she needs to

> [w]ait for the dust of reading to settle; for the conflict and the questioning to die down; walk, talk, pull the dead petals from a rose, or fall asleep. Then suddenly without our willing it, for it is thus that Nature undertakes these transitions, the book will return, but differently (Woolf, *The Common Reader II* 266).

***

Great arts - either visual arts such as paintings or verbal arts such as literature, make us question the meaning of life, love, passion, and death. ‘Life, life, life, what art thou’ (Woolf 257)? Orlando asks himself, and asks this question to the readers. Through a biography, a life does want to be read. Just like great works of art - even the painters were long gone, their ‘radiance’ (qtd. in Bailey 251), as Proust had it, could still be felt as long as we are still looking at the paintings.

Works Cited

Aragon, Louis. *Paris Peasant*. Trans. Simon Watson Taylor. Boston: Exact Change, 1994.

Bailey, Anthony. *A View of Delft: Vermeer Then and Now*. London: Pimlico, Random House, 2001.

Benjamin, Walter. *Berlin Childhood around 1900*. Trans. Howard Eiland. Cambridge, MA: Harvard University Press, 2006.

---. *Walter Benjamin's Archive: Images, Texts, Signs*. Trans. Esther Leslie. Eds. Ursula Marx, et al. London: Verso, 2007.

Berger, John. *About Looking*. New York: Vintage (a division of Random House), 1991.

Bradbrook, M. C. *Shakespeare and Elizabethan Poetry: A Study of his Earlier Work in Relation to the Poetry of the Time.* London: Chatto and Windus, 1951.

Brontë, Emily. *Wuthering Heights*. London: Penguin, 1994.

Doerr, Anthony. *The Shell Collector: Stories*. London: 4th Estate, 2016.

Dwight, Eleanor. *The Gilded Age: Edith Wharton and her Contemporaries*. New York: Universe Publishing (a division of Rizzoli International Publications), 1996.

Eagleton, Terry. 'Wuthering Heights'. *The Eagleton Reader.* Ed. Stephen Regan. Oxford: Blackwell, 1998.

Fleishman, Avrom. 'To Return to St Ives: Woolf's Autobiographical Writings'. *ELH* 48.3 (1981): 606 - 618.

French, Marilyn. 'The Late Tragedies'. *Shakespearean Tragedy*. Ed. John Drakakis. London: Longman, 1992.

Freud, Sigmund. *The Interpretation of Dreams (Second Part) and On Dreams. The Standard Edition of the Complete*

Psychological Works of Sigmund Freud, Volume V (1900 - 1901). Trans. James Strachey, in collaboration with Anna Freud, assisted by Alix Strachey and Alan Tyson. London: Hogarth Press and the Institute of Psycho-Analysis, 1973.

Gilloch, Graeme. *Myth & Metropolis: Walter Benjamin and the City*. Oxford: Polity Blackwell, 1997.

Grace, Sherrill E. 'Quest for the Peaceable Kingdom: Urban / Rural Codes in Roy, Laurence, and Atwood'. *Women Writers and the City*. Ed. Susan Merrill Squier. Knoxville: The University of Tennessee Press, 1984.

Hall, Michael. *The Harold Samuel Collection: A Guide to the Dutch and Flemish Pictures at Mansion House*. London: Paul Holberton, 2012.

Homans, Margaret. 'Repression and Sublimation of Nature in *Wuthering Heights'*. *PMLA* 93.1 (1978): 9 - 19.

McKibben, Robert C. 'The Image of the Book in *Wuthering Heights'*. *Nineteenth-Century Fiction* 15.2 (1960): 159 - 169.

Meyers, Jeffrey. *Painting and the Novel*. Manchester: Manchester University Press, 1975.

Pamuk, Orhan. *Istanbul: Memories of a City*. Trans. Maurren Freely. London: Faber and Faber, 2006.

---. *The Red-haired Woman*. Trans. Ekin Oklap. London: Faber & Faber, 2017.

Riu, Carmen Perez. 'Two Gothic Feminist Texts: Emily Bronte's "Wuthering Heights" and the Film, "The Piano", by Jane Campion'. *Atlantis* 22.1 (2000): 163 - 173.

Sartre, Jean-Paul. *Words*. Trans. Irene Clephane. London: Penguin, 2000.

Shakespeare, William. *The Riverside Shakespeare*. Ed. G. Blakemore Evans. Boston: Houghton Mifflin, 1974.

Shore, Elizabeth M. 'Virginia Woolf, Proust, and *Orlando*'. *Comparative Literature* 31.3 (1979): 232 - 245.

Wharton, Edith. *Summer*. London: Penguin, 1993.

---. *The Age of Innocence*. Cambridge: Cambridge University Press, 1995.

Woolf, Virginia. *Women and Writing*. Michèle Barrett, ed. New York: Harvest (Harcourt Brace & Company), 1980.

---. *To the Lighthouse*. London: Penguin, 2000.

---. *Orlando: A Biography*. Oxford: Oxford University Press, 2000.

---. *The Common Reader II*. Andrew McNeillie, ed. London: Vintage, 2003.

語言文學類　PG2705　文學視界134

The Condition of Language

作　　者／林孜郁（Tzu Yu Allison Lin）
責任編輯／尹懷君
圖文排版／蔡忠翰
封面設計／劉肇昇

發 行 人／宋政坤
法律顧問／毛國樑　律師
出版發行／秀威資訊科技股份有限公司
114台北市內湖區瑞光路76巷65號1樓
電話：+886-2-2796-3638　傳真：+886-2-2796-1377
http://www.showwe.com.tw
劃撥帳號／19563868　戶名：秀威資訊科技股份有限公司
讀者服務信箱：service@showwe.com.tw
展售門市／國家書店（松江門市）
104台北市中山區松江路209號1樓
電話：+886-2-2518-0207　傳真：+886-2-2518-0778
網路訂購／秀威網路書店：https://store.showwe.tw
國家網路書店：https://www.govbooks.com.tw

2021年12月　BOD一版
定價：200元

讀者回函卡